D1368636

A TEMPLAR BOOK

Specially produced for Book Express, Inc.,
Airport Business Center, 29 Kripes Road, East Granby, CT 06026.

USA display marketing rights are exclusive to Book Express

Devised and procuced by the Templar Company plc
Pippbrook Mill, London Road, Dorking, Surrey, Great Britain.

This edition copyright © 1992 by the Templar Company plc

All rights reserved. No part of this publication may be reproduced,
stored in a retrieval system, or transmitted in any form or by any means,
electronic, mechanical, photocopying, recording or otherwise,
without the prior permission of the publisher and copyright holder.

Printed and bound in Italy
ISBN 1-870956-08-7

Bedtime Book

Book Express
Quality and Value in Every Book...

Nursery Rhymes

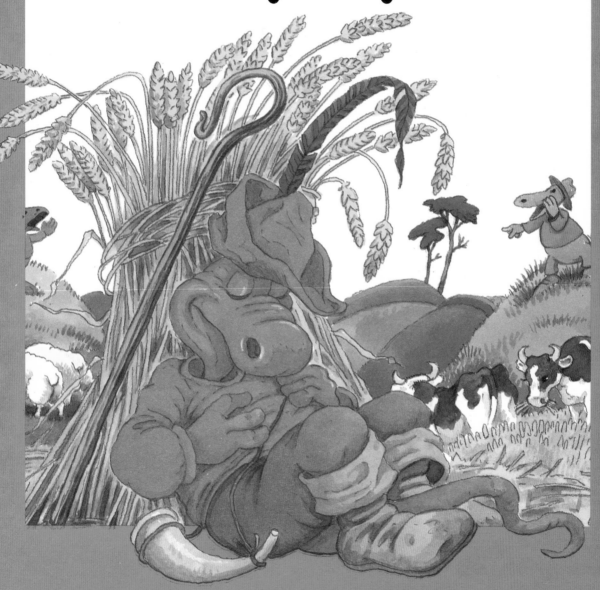

Goosey, Goosey, Gander

Goosey, goosey , gander,
Whither shall I wander?
Upstairs and downstairs
And in my lady's chamber.
There I met an old man
Who would not say his prayers.
I took him by the left leg
And threw him down the stairs.

Hickory, Dickory, Dock

Hickory, dickory, dock,
The mouse ran up the clock.
The clock struck one,
The mouse ran down,
Hickory, dickory dock.

Humpty Dumpty

Humpty Dumpty sat on a wall,
Humpty Dumpty had a great fall;
All the King's horses and all the King's men
Couldn't put Humpty together again.

The Lion and the Unicorn

The Lion and the Unicorn were fighting for the crown;
The Lion beat the Unicorn all round about the town.

Some gave them white bread, some gave them brown;
Some gave them plum cake, and drummed them out
of town.

Hark, hark, the dogs do bark

Hark, hark, the dogs do bark,
The beggars are coming to town;
Some in rags, and some in jags,
And some in velvet gowns.

Pussy cat, pussy cat, where have you been?

Pussy cat, pussy cat, where have you been?
I've been to London to see the Queen.
Pussy cat, pussy cat, what did you there?
I frightened a little mouse under her chair.

Little Boy Blue

Little boy blue, come blow your horn;
The cow's in the meadow, the sheep's in the corn;
Where is the boy who looks after the sheep?
He's under the haycock fast a-sleep.
Will you wake him? No, not I!
For if I do, he's sure to cry.

Cock-a-doodle-doo!

Cock-a-doodle-doo!
My dame has lost her shoe,
My master's lost his fiddling stick,
And doesn't know what to do.

Cock-a-doodle-doo!
What is my dame to do?
Till master finds his fiddling stick,
She'll dance without her shoe.

Cock-a-doodle-doo!
My dame has found her shoe,
And master's found his fiddling stick,
Sing cock-a-doodle-doo.

Cock-a-doodle-doo!
My dame will dance with you,
While master fiddles his fiddling stick,
For dame and doodle doo.

If all the seas were one sea

If all the seas were one sea,
What a *great* sea that would be!
And if all the trees were one tree,
What a *great* tree that would be!
And if all the axes were one axe,
What a *great* axe that would be!
And if all the men were one man,
What a *great* man he would be!
And if the *great* man took the *great* axe,
And cut down the *great* tree,
And let it fall into the *great* sea,
What a splish, splash *that* would be!

I saw three ships come sailing by

I saw three ships come sailing by,
Come sailing by, come sailing by,
I saw three ships come sailing by,
On New Year's Day in the morning.

And what do you think was in them then,
Was in them then, was in them then?
And what do you think was in them then
On New Year's Day in the morning?

Three pretty girls were in them then,
Were in them then, were in them then,
Three pretty girls were in them then,
On New Year's Day in the morning.

One could whistle, and one could sing,
And one could play on the violin,
Such joy there was at my wedding,
On New Year's Day in the morning.

Polly put the kettle on

Polly put the kettle on,
Polly put the kettle on,
Polly put the kettle on,
We'll all have tea.

Sukey take it off again,
Sukey take it off again,
Sukey take it off again,
They've all gone away.

Peter Piper

Peter Piper picked a peck of pickled pepper;
A peck of pickled pepper Peter Piper picked;
If Peter Piper picked a peck of pickled pepper,
Where's the peck of pickled pepper Peter Piper picked?

Pease-porridge hot

Pease-porridge hot,
Pease-porridge cold,
Pease-porridge in the pot,
Nine days old.
Spell me that in four letters.
I will.
T-H-A-T.

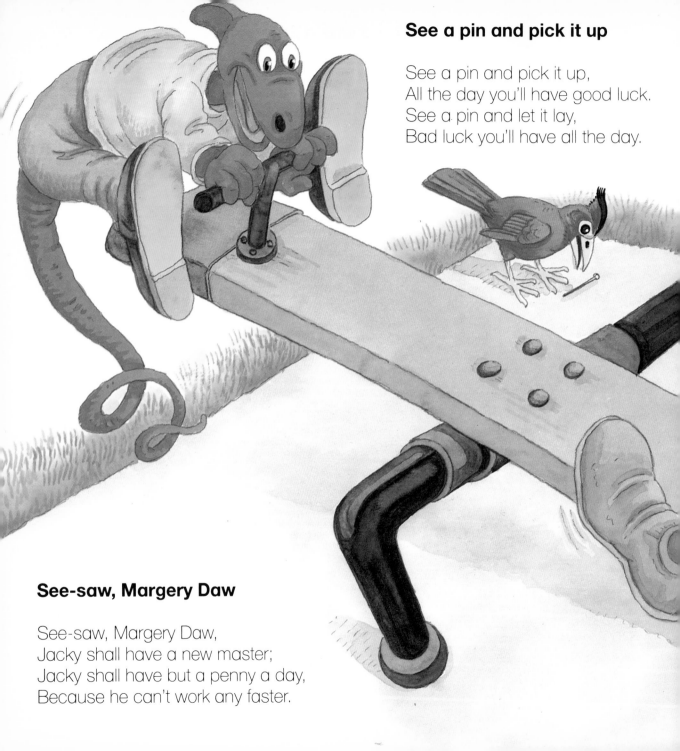

See a pin and pick it up

See a pin and pick it up,
All the day you'll have good luck.
See a pin and let it lay,
Bad luck you'll have all the day.

See-saw, Margery Daw

See-saw, Margery Daw,
Jacky shall have a new master;
Jacky shall have but a penny a day,
Because he can't work any faster.

There was a little girl

There was a little girl, and she had a little curl
Right in the middle of her forehead;
When she was good she was very, very good,
But when she was bad she was horrid.

Here we go round the mulberry bush

Here we go round the mulberry bush,
The mulberry bush, the mulberry bush,
Here we go round the mulberry bush,
On a cold and frosty morning.

This is the way we clap our hands,
Clap our hands, clap our hands,
This is the way we clap our hands,
On a cold and frosty morning.

Boys and girls, come out to play

Boys and girls, come out to play,
The moon doth shine as bright as day,
Leave your supper, and leave your sleep,
And come with your playfellows into the street.
Come with a whoop, come with a call,
Come with a good will, or come not at all.
Up the ladder and down the wall,
A halfpenny loaf will serve us all.
You find milk, and I'll find flour,
And we"ll have pudding in half an hour.

Ring around the Rosie

Ring around the Rosie,
A pocket full of posies,
A-tishoo! A-tishoo!
We all fall down.

Hey diddle, diddle

Hey diddle, diddle,
The cat and the fiddle,
The cow jumped over the moon;
The little dog laughed
To see such fun,
And the dish ran away with the spoon.

Twinkle, twinkle, little star

Twinkle, twinkle, little star,
How I wonder what you are!
Up above the moon so high,
Like a diamond in the sky.

There was an old woman tossed up in a basket

There was an old woman tossed up in a basket,
Ninety times as high as the moon:
And where she was going, I couldn't but ask her,
For in her hand she carried a broom.

"Old woman, old woman, old woman," quoth I,
"Wither, O wither, O wither so high?"
"To sweep the cobwebs off the sky!"
"Shall I go with you?" "Aye, by-and-by."

Come, let's to bed

"Come, let's to bed,"
Says Sleepy-head;
"Tarry a while," says Slow.
"Put on the pot,"
Says the Greedy one,
"Let's sup before we go."

Jack be nimble

Jack be nimble,
Jack be quick,
Jack jump over
The candlestick.

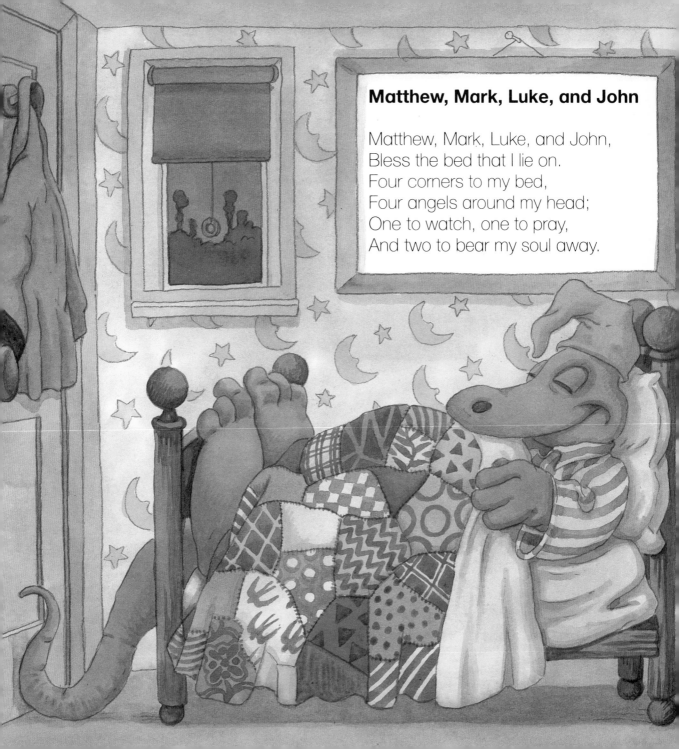

Matthew, Mark, Luke, and John

Matthew, Mark, Luke, and John,
Bless the bed that I lie on.
Four corners to my bed,
Four angels around my head;
One to watch, one to pray,
And two to bear my soul away.

Favorite Fairy Tales

The Princess and the Pea

Once upon a time, there was a very fussy prince who would only marry a fussy princess. The king and queen looked everywhere for a suitable bride, but the prince rejected them all. He was determined to find a princess who was so delicate that a speck of dust would make her scream, and so sensitive that the breeze from a fly's wing would give her a cold.

One evening during a terrible thunderstorm, the king heard someone knocking at the palace door. He opened it to discover a beautiful girl soaking wet from head to toe.

"Please let me in," she said. "I am a princess."
The king and queen decided to find out if she
would be fussy enough for their son. They prepared a
special bed of 20 mattresses under which they
placed a small pea.

The next morning the girl looked very tired.
"I tossed and turned all night," she complained.
"There was something hard in my bed and I could not sleep."

The king and queen knew at once that she was the princess for their son and the prince was overjoyed to discover someone else as fussy as himself. They got married that very day and lived happily ever after.

Aladdin and the Magic Lamp

Once upon a time, a wicked magician forced his poor nephew, Aladdin, down into a deep, dark cave to find him a magic lamp. However, Aladdin also found and collected a lot of other treasures while he was there, making him late. This made his uncle so angry that he cast an evil spell to shut Aladdin in the cave for ever.

Luckily, Aladdin found a magic ring inside the cave which, when rubbed, produced a genie to grant his every wish.

"Take me home," ordered Aladdin and, suddenly, he and his newly-found riches were back home.

Then, one day Aladdin met a beautiful princess and fell in love with her. However, her father would not let Aladdin even see her until he could prove his wealth. By now, most of the riches from the cave were gone because Aladdin had to use them to buy food. He summoned the Genie of the Ring, but he could not help poor Aladdin.

"Speak to the Genie of the Lamp, he will help you," said the Genie of the Ring to Aladdin.

After searching high and low, Aladdin found the old lamp that had come from the cave and when he rubbed it another genie appeared. The Genie of the Lamp gave Aladdin so much wealth that he was able to impress the powerful king and gain permission to marry his daughter. Aladdin and the princess lived happily ever after.

Jack and the Beanstalk

Once upon a time, there was a poor widow who had a son named Jack. One day she sent Jack to the market to sell their cow. On the way, Jack met a man and sold him the cow for five magic beans. Jack's mother was very angry. She threw the beans out of the window and sent Jack to bed without his supper.

The magic beans started to grow and soon there was a giant beanstalk outside the cottage. Jack climbed all the way to the top where there stood a giant's castle. Inside, Jack found three bags of gold. Quickly, he ran back down the beanstalk with them.

However, soon the gold ran out so Jack climbed back up the beanstalk again. This time he saw the towering giant who was busy eating his dinner. On the table nearby was a beautiful hen that layed golden eggs. Quickly, Jack grabbed the hen and, with the giant right behind him, Jack ran back down the beanstalk and got home safely.

By now Jack was very curious about the giant's treasures. He climbed the beanstalk again. This time the giant was fast asleep, so Jack took a magical singing harp for his mother. Suddenly, the giant roared awake. "Thump, thump, thump," chased the giant as Jack ran down the beanstalk.

"Quick, mother, get the axe," Jack called, and together they chopped down the beanstalk. It crashed to the ground along with the giant.

And so Jack and his mother lived happily ever after with the hen that layed golden eggs and the magical harp that sang.

Sleeping Beauty

Once upon a time, there was a beautiful princess named Aurora. When she was born, her parents asked all the fairies in the kingdom to be her godmothers. However, they neglected one fairy who became so angry that she cast an evil spell upon Aurora.

"One day Aurora will prick her finger on a poison spindle – and die!" cried the wicked fairy.

Luckily, one last fairy godmother had yet to give Aurora her birthday gift.

"I cannot undo the evil spell," she said, "but I can change it. Aurora will prick her finger, but she will not die. She will fall into a deep sleep for a hundred years, only to be awakened by a kiss from a prince."

One day, as Aurora was approaching her 16th birthday, she discovered a spindle in a dark and musty room in the palace. Aurora touched it and pricked her finger. She fell instantly into a deep sleep and the good fairies put the rest of the castle to sleep so that Aurora would not be alone.

One hundred years later, a brave, young prince
who had heard the legend of the sleeping princess
went in search of Aurora.

"Such a sleeping beauty, she is," thought the
prince when he found her, and then he bent down to
kiss her.

Instantly, the evil spell was broken! Princess Aurora and the rest of the palace awoke. Aurora fell in love with the handsome prince. They were married that very day and lived happily ever after.

A Dinosaur's Dream

Once
upon a time,
a dinosaur
dreamed...

He dreamed he was a bird,
flying in the sky.

The bird flew and flew
until he came to a field
full of yellow flowers...

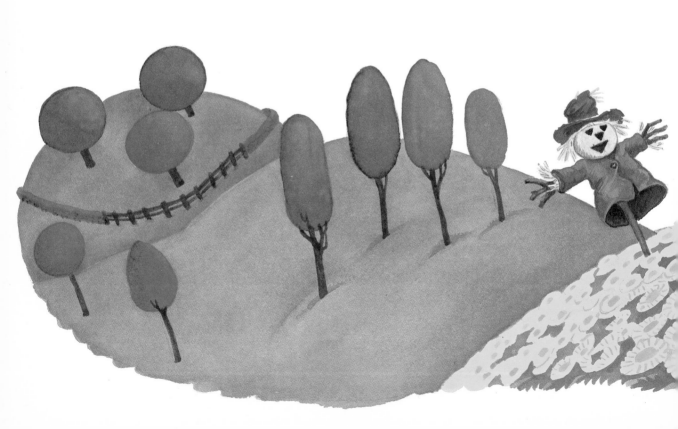

Then he dreamed he was a
flower waving in the wind.

The wind whisked him away,
and he floated to the sea...

He dreamed he was a fish,
swimming beneath the waves.

The fish swam and swam
until winter came...

Then he dreamed
he was a snowman,
with a carrot for his nose.

The snowman
shivered in the cold
until the sun came out...

Then he dreamed he was a
butterfly, flying in the sun.

He fluttered over
fields and
meadows...

Until it was night,
and darkness fell...

Then he dreamed
he was a dinosaur
tucked up in bed.

And the dinosaur dreamed...

Dinosaur
Do's and Dont's

What do dinosaurs do?

Dinosaurs DO eat
up their breakfast...

Dinosaurs DON'T
spill crumbs on the floor.

Dinosaurs DO
tidy their
bedrooms...

Dinosaurs DON'T leave their toys all over the floor.

Dinosaurs DO
tie their shoelaces
and button their coats...

Dinosaurs DON'T jump in puddles on the way to school.

Dinosaurs DO
clean their teeth...

Dinosaurs DON'T
eat too many sweets.

Dinosaurs DO
go to bed
when they are told...

Dinosaurs DON'T
stay up late watching TV...

At least, not very often.